P9-EJZ-206

THE ORANGE BOOK

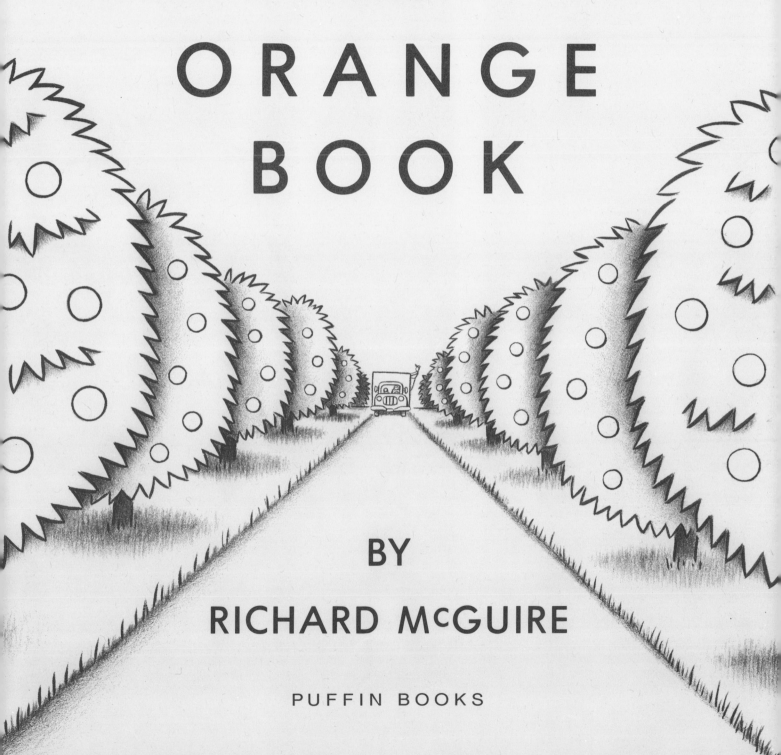

BY

RICHARD McGUIRE

PUFFIN BOOKS

There once was a tree with fourteen oranges.

One was sent to a sick friend.

Two was used in a juggling act.

Three went to art school.

Four was squeezed for the juice.

Five was served with fortune cookies.

Six was used for marmalade.

Seven was divided among the crew.

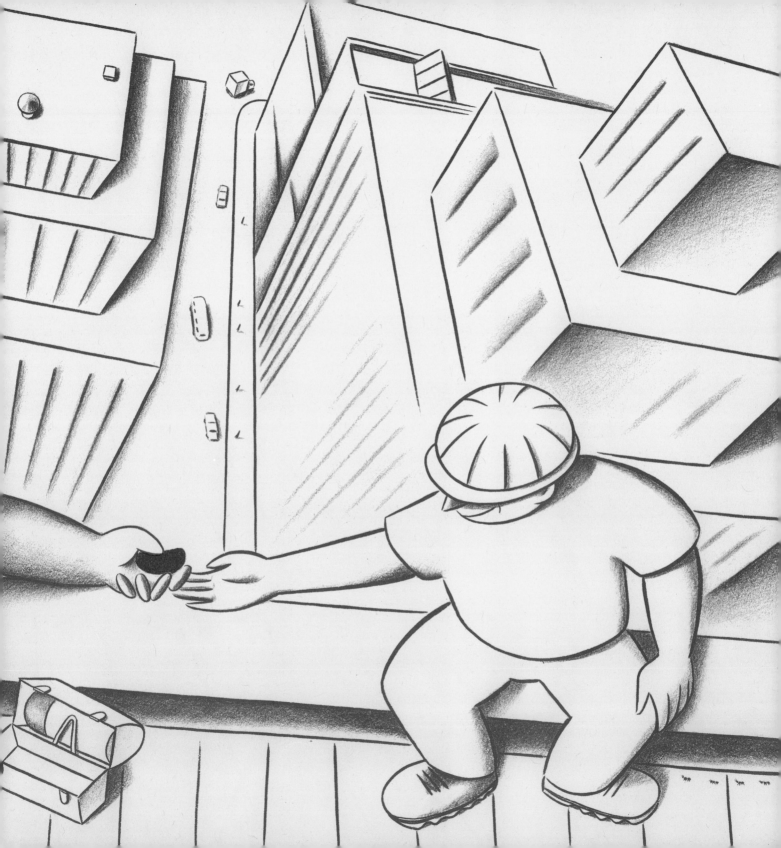

Eight rolled overboard.

Nine was used in a strange experiment.

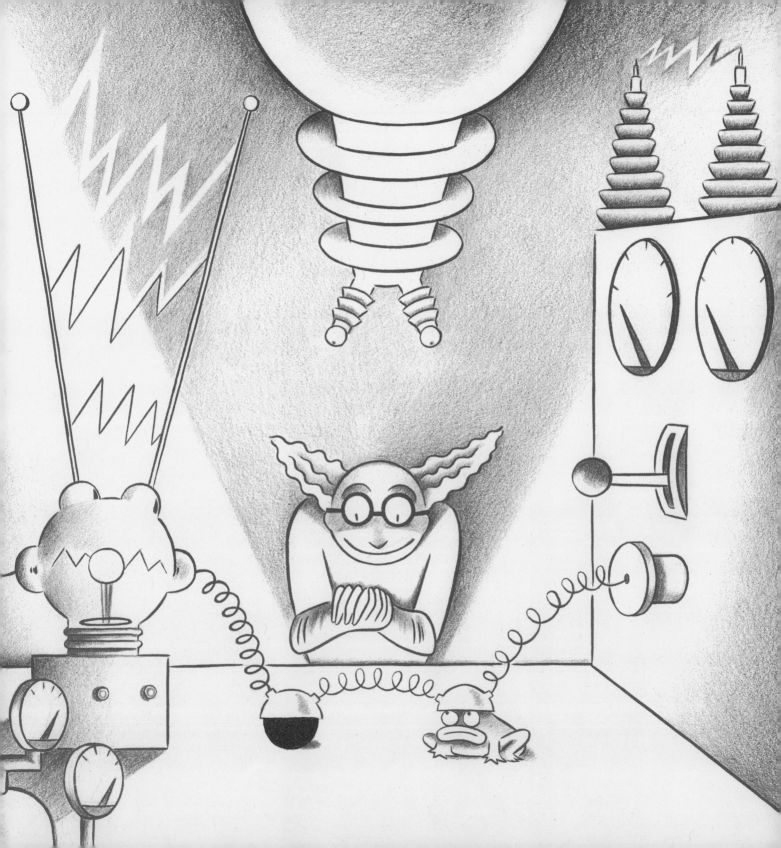

Ten was eaten by a famous pianist.

Eleven ended up on the train tracks.

Twelve was on TV...

...Thirteen was not as lucky.

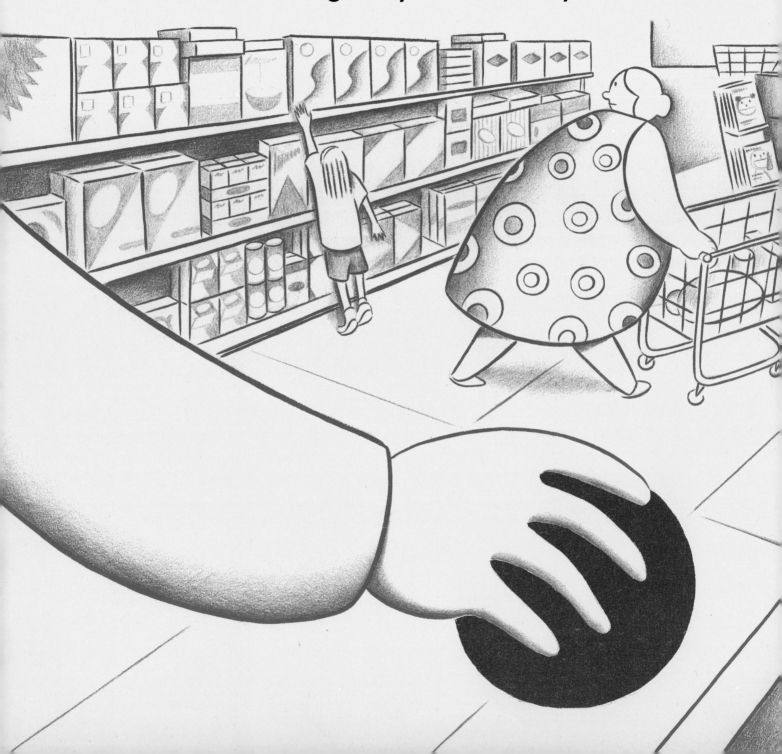

...and may be the next one you eat.

For Mom and Modigliani

Special thanks to Howard, Liz, Billy, and Paul

PUFFIN BOOKS
Published by the Penguin Group
Penguin Books USA Inc., 375 Hudson Street, New York, New York 10014, U.S.A.
Penguin Books Ltd, 27 Wrights Lane, London W8 5TZ, England
Penguin Books Australia Ltd, Ringwood, Victoria, Australia
Penguin Books Canada Ltd, 10 Alcorn Avenue, Toronto, Ontario, Canada M4V 3B2
Penguin Books (N.Z.) Ltd, 182-190 Wairau Road, Auckland 10, New Zealand

Penguin Books Ltd, Registered Offices: Harmondsworth, Middlesex, England

First published in the United States of America by Universe Publishing,
a division of Rizzoli International Publications, Inc., 1992
Published in Puffin Books, 1994

1 3 5 7 9 10 8 6 4 2

LIBRARY OF CONGRESS CATALOGING-IN-PUBLICATION DATA
McGuire, Richard.
The orange book / by Richard McGuire.   p.   cm.
"First published in the United States of America by Children's Universe . . . 1992"—T.p. verso.
Summary: Fourteen oranges, fresh from their tree, make their way in the world and
end up in various places including art school, vaudeville, and television.
ISBN 0-14-055342-8
[1. Orange—Fiction. 2. Counting.] I. Title.
PZ7.M4786215O74 1994 [E]—dc20 94-15031 CIP AC

Printed in the United States of America
Design by Richard McGuire